The Perfect Monster

SALLY GRINDLEY

ILLUSTRATED BY
ERICA-JANE WATERS

KINGFISHER

BOSTON

KINGFISHER
a Houghton Mifflin Company imprint
222 Berkeley Street
Boston, Massachusetts 02116
www.houghtonmifflinbooks.com

First published in 2005
4 6 8 10 9 7 5 3

LIBRARY OF CONGRESS CATALOGING-IN-PUBLICATION DATA
Grindley, Sally.
The perfect monster/Sally Grindley; illustrated by Erica-Jane Waters.
p. cm.—(I am reading)
Summary: Mungus Bigfoot is the most gruesome, scariest monster in his class, but when he is ordered to teach
sweet little Emily Twinkletoes how to act like a proper monster, she teaches him a lesson instead.

[Monsters—Fiction. 2. Individuality—Fiction. 3. Behavior—Fiction. 4. Schools—Fiction.] I. Waters, Erica-Jane,
ill. II. Title. III. Series.
PZ7.G88446Pdu 2005
[Fic]—dc22   2005027420
ISBN 0-7534-5858-6
ISBN 978-07534-5858-7

Printed in Canada
3TR/0106/TCL/SGCH(SGCH)/80CAS/C

Contents

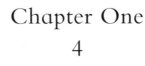

Chapter One

From the first day of his life Mungus
Bigfoot was THE PERFECT MONSTER.
When he was born, he screamed so
loudly—AAAAAAGH!—that all of the
windows in the hospital broke. CRASH!
"What a perfect entrance!" everyone said.

When his mother
changed his diapers,
he always soaked
her—WEEEE!
"What a perfect shot!"
everyone said.

When aunties held their fingers out for him to suck, he bit them—EEEK! "What perfect teeth!" everyone said. His parents couldn't have been more proud.

When Mungus Bigfoot was two, he won
a prize for scaring old ladies at bus stops.

When he was three,
he won a competition
to find the loudest
GRRRR!

When he was four, he
came first in a contest
to see who could
throw their food
the farthest.

When he was five,
he went to school
and was declared
the dirtiest, smelliest
monster in his class.

When he was six,
he knew more rude
words than all of
his classmates put
together.

When he was seven, he was the youngest monster ever to pass his "Monster in the Closet" test.

When he was eight, he was awarded the highest grades ever on his "Monster Under the Bed" test.

Every year he was told, "Mungus Bigfoot, you are THE PERFECT MONSTER."

Chapter Two

Then, one day, Mungus Bigfoot was given a very special job.

"I want you to show Emily Twinkletoes how to be a good monster," said the Head Monster at his school.

Mungus was horrified.

"But Emily Twinkletoes is THE WORST MONSTER EVER!" he protested. "She couldn't even scare a fly!"

"If anyone can help her, you can," the
Head Monster said. "She'll listen to you."
"I won't obey you," growled Mungus.
"For once, you will," ordered the Head
Monster, "or you will be expelled."

Mungus Bigfoot couldn't believe his ears.
Expelled! He was THE PERFECT
MONSTER. They couldn't expel him!

Chapter Three

Emily Twinkletoes was put next to him in class.

"You're so perfect, Mungus Bigfoot," she whispered. "I wish I could be like you."

"Then try a little harder," growled Mungus.

"I've tried, but I'm just not good at it," said Emily with a sigh.

"Throw this bag of flour at the teacher," said Mungus.

"Ooo, I couldn't," said Emily. "That would be naughty."

"You're supposed to be naughty," snapped Mungus. "Watch this."

He hurled the bag of flour and hit the
teacher right in the face—SPLAT!
"Who did that?" shouted the teacher.

"Emily Twinkletoes," Mungus replied.

"What a great shot!" said the teacher.

"Ten out of ten!"

"Oh, but it wasn't me," cried Emily.

"Shhh!" said Mungus. "Now shout out
the worst rude word you can think of."
Emily turned bright pink. "Ooo, I
couldn't," she said with a giggle.
"Shout it," growled Mungus.
Emily took a deep breath. "Poo!" she
whispered.

Mungus gave her a nasty look, and then he yelled out, "Stinkwhiffysmellofeet!"

"Who said that?" demanded the teacher.

"Emily Twinkletoes," said Mungus.

"What a great rude word!" said the teacher. "Ten out of ten!"

"Oh, but it wasn't me," cried Emily.

Mungus felt like tearing his hair out.

At recess Emily asked him to play hopscotch with her.

"No way," said Mungus. "We're going to frighten the nursery monsters."

"Ooo, I couldn't do that!" squealed Emily.

At lunchtime Emily asked him to jump
rope with her.

"No way," said Mungus. "We're
going to throw tomatoes at the
lunch monsters."

"Ooo, I couldn't do that!" squealed
Emily.

"What can you do then?" groaned
Mungus.

"I know all my times tables," said
Emily, "and I can write in cursive, and I
can read all the words in the dictionary,
and I know how to be nice."

Mungus gasped with horror. "But that's terrible," he howled. "Your parents must be so ashamed of you."

"They are," nodded Emily. "But you're going to help me make them proud." Then she gave Mungus such a beautiful great big smile that he couldn't help smiling back.

Chapter Four

Over the next few weeks Mungus tried
everything he could think of to turn
Emily into a better monster.

He taught her how to scream a really scary scream.

But instead of screaming, Emily taught him how to sing.

He taught her all the rude words that he knew. But instead of saying them, Emily taught him how to spell them.

Stink
whiffy
smello
feet

RUDE WORDS

MONSTERS

He showed her how to hide behind
bushes and jump out to frighten
passersby. But instead of frightening
anyone, Emily showed Mungus how
to make a daisy chain.

He showed her how to hide under a bed,
ready to scare a sleeping child.

But Emily snuggled up to him and fell
fast asleep.

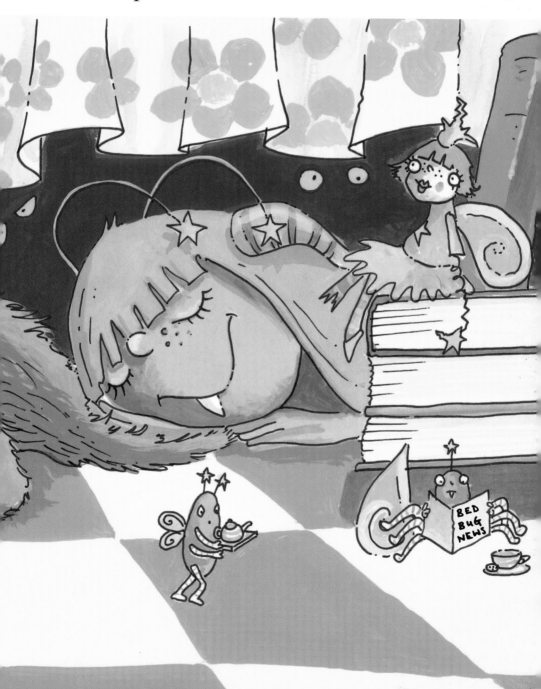

The worst thing was that Mungus began to like Emily the way she was.

"You're so different from any other monster I've ever met," he said.

"I know," she said with a giggle.

"It's terrible, isn't it? But you're helping

me change, aren't you, Mungus?"

Mungus made a face and mumbled,

"I think you might be changing me."

Emily looked shocked. "But that's awful!

You can't change, Mungus.

You're everybody's hero."

"And if I don't make you into a better

monster, I'll be expelled," Mungus sighed.

Emily looked even more shocked.

"I didn't know that," she whispered.

Chapter Five

The next day began with a lesson in
making faces.

"I want you to make the scariest face
imaginable," the teacher said to the class.

"I'm going to try really hard today,"
Emily whispered to Mungus.

Mungus looked at her beaming smile and
shook his head.

"You can't make a scary face," he said.

"You wait and see," grinned Emily.

One by one, the monsters made the worst

faces they could.

When it came to Mungus's turn, he made such a horrible face that all of the other monsters cheered.

"What a truly horrible face!" cried the teacher. "Ten out of ten."

Then Emily Twinkletoes leaped to her feet.

"Look at this," she cried.

And she made such a terrible face that
all of the other monsters cowered in their
boots.

"What a horrible, awful, nasty, foul, gruesome, terrible face!" cried the teacher. "One hundred out of one hundred!"

"I did it!" screamed Emily. "Did you see me, Mungus?"

Mungus nodded his head. "Well done, Emily," he said. But he looked very sad. Emily had made the worst face he had ever seen, but he didn't like to see her doing it.

During that day
Emily made the
worst slime pie
that anyone had
ever tasted.

She came first in
the class for scary
leaps off of tables.

And she came
first for making
the rudest noises.

When she hurled a mud pie straight into the face of the Head Monster, the Head Monster cheered and patted Mungus on the back.

"Well done, Mungus," he said. "You've turned Emily Twinkletoes into a perfect little monster."

Instead of being pleased, Mungus felt
terrible. He walked sadly home.
Suddenly, he heard his name.
"Wait for me, Mungus."
Emily ran up to him and slipped her
hand into his.

"Thank you for helping me, Mungus," she said.

Mungus shook his head. "You were perfect the way you were, and now I've spoiled you."

"Was I too good at being bad?" asked Emily quietly.

"What do you mean?" said Mungus.

"I forgot to tell you that I'm a wonderful actress," she grinned.

"You mean you haven't really changed?" asked Mungus.

"Not at all," Emily said with a giggle.

"I have, though," sighed Mungus.

"Yes, you have," said Emily solemnly.

And then she clapped her hands and burst out laughing. "You're more perfect than ever now. My perfect monster."

About the author and illustrator

Sally Grindley is an award-winning author with many books to her name. She had a whale of a time writing *The Perfect Monster*. "I got the giggles thinking about what a monster would have to do to be perfect and how difficult it would be to teach a hopeless monster." Sally has also written the *I Am Reading* book *Captain Pepper's Pets*.

Erica-Jane Waters paints lots of pictures, mostly for children's books. She says, "I'm a complete Mungus—I'm always covered in paint and occasionally throw food. In my spare time I like getting muddy in my garden, where I grow strange vegetables. Last year I grew green, warty pumpkins!"

Strategies for Independent Readers

Predict
Think about the cover, illustrations, and the title of the book. What do you think this book will be about? While you are reading think about what may happen next and why.

Monitor
As you read ask yourself if what you're reading makes sense. If it doesn't, reread, look at the illustrations, or read ahead.

Question
Ask yourself questions about important ideas in the story such as what the characters might do or what you might learn.

Phonics
If there is a word that you do not know, look carefully at the letters, sounds, and word parts that you do know. Blend the sounds to read the word. Ask yourself if this is a word you know. Does it make sense in the sentence?

Summarize
Think about the characters, the setting where the story takes place, and the problem the characters faced in the story. Tell the important ideas in the beginning, middle, and end of the story.

Evaluate
Ask yourself questions like: Did you like the story? Why or why not? How did the author make the story come alive? How did the author make the story fun to read? How well did you understand the story? Maybe you can understand it better if you read it again!